Also by Colin Dann

Novels
THE ANIMALS OF FARTHING WOOD
IN THE GRIP OF WINTER
FOX'S FEUD
THE FOX CUB BOLD
THE SIEGE OF WHITE DEER PARK
IN THE PATH OF THE STORM
THE BATTLE FOR THE PARK

Picture Books
THE FLIGHT FROM FARTHING WOOD

First published in Great Britain 1993 by William Heinemann Ltd
an imprint of Reed Consumer Books Limited
Michelin House, 81 Fulham Road, London SW3 6RB
and Auckland, Melbourne, Singapore and Toronto
Reprinted 1993
Reprinted 1994 (twice)
Copyright © 1993 Colin Dann
Illustrations copyright © 1993 Reed International Books Limited

ISBN 0 434 96375 5

Printed and bound by **GRAPHICOM,** Vicenza

The
ANIMALS
of
FARTHING
WOOD

A story by Colin Dann

Illustrated by
Stuart Trotter

HEINEMANN

The End of the Wood

Dusk was falling on Farthing Wood as Badger left his comfortable underground home. He sniffed the dry air. There had been no rain for weeks and underfoot the soil was rock hard. Badger noticed Tawny Owl sitting on a low branch nearby. He trotted over.

"Still no rain," said Badger. "And how hot it seems."

"I have some bad news," Tawny Owl remarked bluntly. "The men have filled in our pond." Her huge eyes stared at Badger's striped face.

The old animal looked alarmed. "But this is serious, Owl," he said. "Where shall we go to drink now?"

Tawny Owl's head turned to watch another friend, Fox, approaching. "Perhaps he can tell you," she suggested. "Fox will know if anyone does."

Fox greeted them, then shook his head at Badger's enquiry. "No, there's not a drop of water left anywhere," he said. "And the humans have cut down more trees. Our wood is being destroyed bit by bit."

"How long before —" faltered Badger.

"Before it's all gone?" Tawny Owl finished for him. "Could be this summer. Humans work fast when they're destroying things."

Fox nodded. "We know that only too well. Three quarters of the wood have gone already. Brick and concrete have taken its place. We've been driven back and driven back. Only at nightfall is there any peace."

"But with each daybreak," said Owl, "the machines return. Tearing, ripping, crushing …"

"Soon we shall be driven out altogether," Fox continued. "We shall have to run."

"Run?" echoed Badger. "But where to?"

"I don't know," Fox said. "It needs all the creatures in the wood to put their heads together. There must be an Assembly. Everyone must attend and put forward their ideas. Large and small, we're all of us in the same plight."

"Exactly," said Badger. "We must round up the whole of Farthing Wood, pass the word around."

"Your set is the ideal meeting-place," Fox said to Badger. "We shall be safe underground."

"And it's roomy and clean," Badger said proudly.

"Tomorrow at midnight, then," said Fox. "Owl will inform the birds. Badger and I will tell the beasts."

Tawny Owl rustled her wings. "Can't see how birds can go underground," she complained.

"You'll manage," Fox said simply. "Come on, there's no time to lose."

The moon was shining brightly as Badger and Fox separated. Each took a different direction. They were the largest and most powerful creatures in Farthing Wood, so they had to reassure the more timid animals that they would be in no danger from attack. In Badger's set predators and prey would be mingled together.

"At an Assembly everyone is bound by the Oath of Common Safety," Badger told the rabbits, who were very nervous. The rabbits told the hares.

Fox found Weasel and the hedgehogs. "Midnight tomorrow. Badger's set. Spread the word."

The hedgehogs told the fieldmice and the mice told the voles. Weasel told the squirrels. The last to be told was Adder.

"Don't forget the Oath," Fox reminded the snake. "There's to be no hunting."

"Of course not," Adder hissed with a leer. "I wouldn't dream of it."

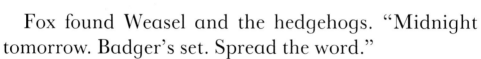

The appointed time arrived. Badger had made sure his set was spotless. From the hedgerows he had gathered glow-worms to light the dark tunnels and chambers. He waited for the first arrival. This was Mole who had dug a passage from his own underground home directly into Badger's main chamber.

Badger greeted his little friend and told him to make himself at home. "I'm going to the exit to watch for the others," he added.

Some came singly. Some came in small groups. Badger directed them into the set's dark interior. Tawny Owl brought Kestrel and a pair of pheasants. The birds walked into the tunnel. Adder arrived late. Badger scolded her.

"Well, someone had to be last," she pointed out.

At the end of the tunnel in the Assembly Chamber the animals began to discuss the situation. All of them were aware of the threat hanging over them.

"Our main concern is to find water," Badger said. "We can't survive long without it. We all need to help one another. So don't be afraid to speak up if you have an idea. Size and strength are forgotten at a time like this."

The smaller animals murmured amongst themselves but none could think of a plan. Badger, Fox and Tawny Owl scanned the circle of faces.

Weasel said, "What about you birds? You cover a wider area than we land animals. Can any of you say where the nearest water is to be found?"

"My mate and I," said Pheasant, "don't venture outside the wood. We're game birds and liable to be shot at." He almost sounded pleased with their importance.

Badger glared at him. He turned to Kestrel. "You're the greatest traveller, Kestrel. Can you offer any advice?"

"Yes," she answered, "though I don't know how useful it will be to you." Every eye looked at the bird expectantly. "There's a swimming-pool in one of the gardens on the new estate. There's water sufficient for all there."

"There'd be no cover," Fox commented. "It'd be a longish journey there and back and we'd be in the open the whole time."

The Assembly fell silent again. Each creature cudgelled its brains for a way out of the difficulty. Suddenly a voice was heard calling from the tunnel outside. "Hallo! Who's there?"

Weasel ran to look. "It's Toad!" she exclaimed in amazement.

Seconds later the newcomer stumbled into the chamber. "I've been looking all over the place for you all," he croaked. "I thought you'd deserted the wood. Then I heard voices ..."

"Toad, wherever have you been?" Badger cried. "We haven't seen you since last spring. We'd given you up for lost."

"I've been on a long journey," Toad gasped. He looked worn out. "I'll tell you about it when I've recovered a little."

Toad tells his Story

"I was captured, you see," Toad began. "Last spring at the pond. Put into one of those glass things and whisked away to a spot so far distant I didn't know where I was. But I managed to escape and of course I had to make my way back here. Each day, except during the cold months, I headed in the direction of my pond. All along I could feel it drawing me towards it. Little by little, day by day for — oh! so long — I've crept closer. Now I'm here and yet — the pond seems to have disappeared."

"Filled in," Tawny Owl hooted. "By the humans."

"But — but —" Toad spluttered, "they *can't*. It was my home."

"We're all in danger of losing our homes," said Hare, "if we don't die of thirst first."

"There's been a drought for weeks," Badger explained. "We have no water left to drink. That's why we've all gathered."

Toad's woeful expression changed to a more hopeful one. "I have the answer! We must leave and travel to a new home. All of us, together. And I know the very place to go to. It's a great distance, of course. But together we can do it."

The animals chattered excitedly at the news. Some were thrilled by the prospect, some were doubtful.

"What is this place?" asked Fox.

"It's called a Nature Reserve," Toad answered. "I got talking to a group of frogs there when I crossed it on my journey back. It's a sort of private park set aside for the benefit of wild creatures where they can live in peace. The place is called White Deer Park."

"Are there deer in it?" asked Mole.

"Of course there are. Rare white deer who need to be protected. So every other creature in the Park is protected too, because no humans are allowed in it. Except one who looks after the Reserve. He's called the Warden."

"This sounds like Paradise," whispered Badger.

"How far is it? Is it a long journey?" all the smaller animals called out. "Would it be too far for us?"

"Why — no," Toad answered. "I'm only small myself and I've made the journey once, travelling back here. So if I can do it, why not you?"

"That's fighting talk!" cried Badger. "How about it.

everyone? Shall Toad be our guide to a new home?"

There was a deafening chorus of approval.

"Then it's farewell to Farthing Wood and onward to White Deer Park!"

There was a tremendous hubbub as all the animals, overcome by excitement, chattered at once. The youngsters ran around chanting, "White Deer Park! White Deer Park!"

"We must plan for this journey," Badger said to Fox. "It will be dangerous and we shall need a leader." He raised his voice. "Quiet, everyone! We have to choose a leader."

There was no difficulty about that. Fox was the cleverest and most courageous animal and all of them knew it. He accepted their choice humbly.

"Thank you," he said. "Now, Toad, I need to know from you what sort of country we'll be crossing."

"Almost all dangerous," Toad replied. "We must travel by night whenever we can. We begin by aiming for the army land on the other side of the road from the new houses."

"Good. We can all pause to drink from the pool on the way," Fox said. "Owl, Kestrel, we'll need you to spy out the land: Kestrel by day and Owl at night. Will you join us?"

"Certainly we shall," they answered.

"There's one big problem," said Weasel. "We're different-sized animals and travel at different speeds."

"Then we must adapt our pace to suit the slowest member of the party," Fox answered. "Who's that?"

"Mole!" everyone cried.

Mole cringed. He was hurt.

"So be it," said Fox. "Now, Toad, what's after the army land?"

"Farmland first – a lot of it, fields and orchards. That's not too difficult. Then we come to the river. That's where it becomes more hazardous."

"Hm. Well, we'll think about that when the time comes. Now, everybody, get a good feed and a good rest tomorrow. We'll need all our strength. We shall start tomorrow night. Are there any questions?"

"Yes," squeaked a fieldmouse. "On behalf of the smaller animals I'd like to ask for the Oath to be renewed tonight, with everyone present. It'd make us feel more comfortable if we know we're all bound by it."

"A worthy thought," Badger agreed. "We shall call this new Oath the Oath of Mutual Protection. And we must all swear it."

All the creatures did so, one by one.

"Tomorrow night," said Fox, "when the village clock strikes twelve, we meet by the Great Beech at the hedgerow. Then our journey begins."

Mole is Lost

All the next day the bulldozers crashed through Farthing Wood, flattening more of the trees. The animals cowered in their lairs and tunnels, quaking at the sound and longing for darkness. When the noise stopped they went in search of food. As midnight approached they took a last look round at their old homes. Then they ran to meet their companions by the Great Beech.

As the last chime of the clock sounded, Fox counted his party. "One missing," he declared. "Mole."

"Oh no," said Badger. "What can have happened?"

"We can't wait for long," Fox warned. "We must be

through the housing estate by daylight."

"I'm sure I can find him," said Badger. "Give me a little time."

"All right. But be quick, Badger!"

Badger loped away in the direction of his set, looking around for Mole as he went. He reached the set and took the passage leading to the Assembly Chamber. Once in there he put his muzzle to the hole from which Mole had emerged on the previous night. He called his little friend in a loud voice.

"MOLE! ARE YOU THERE?"

There were some scuffles. Badger pushed his head right inside the hole and called again, more loudly.

"Is that you, Badger?" came Mole's voice.

"Yes, of course. For goodness' sake, come out, Mole. You're holding everyone up."

"That's just it," Mole said tearfully. "I'm so slow, I *will* hold everyone up. So I'm not coming."

"Don't be ridiculous," said Badger. "How could we leave you here? You *must* come."

"Everybody said —"

"Never mind that," Badger interrupted. "Nobody is to be left behind. And don't worry, you can climb on my back. I'll carry you."

Mole came forward, trying to stifle his sobs. "Oh Badger, you are kind." He clambered on to Badger's back, gripping the thick hair with his claws. "How can I ever thank you?"

"Don't be silly. Now hold tight. I've got to run." They set off at once and, shortly afterwards, the animals were all together. Mole was welcomed enthusiastically and he brightened up at once. The party was complete.

"Now, Owl, Kestrel, when you're ready," Fox prompted.

The bird scouts took to the air and, below them, the mixed group of animals followed. Fox led with Toad hopping alongside. Behind them were the rabbits, hares and hedgehogs; then Weasel, the squirrels, and the voles and fieldmice. Badger and Mole brought up the rear with adder slithering next to them. They moved as quickly as they could through the hedgerow.

They threaded their way past the silent bulldozers that looked like monsters asleep. As they proceeded Farthing Wood grew smaller and smaller behind them against the starlit sky.

The animals entered the housing estate. Kestrel led them to the garden pool where they drank their fill. The sky was growing pale as they reached the trunk road. On the other side of this lay the comparative safety of the army land. The animals were tired; some were exhausted. They had come a long way. Toad in particular could hardly crawl another step.

"Once we're across," he gasped, "we'll ... find some undergrowth ... and rest. I didn't travel such ... long stages on my ... own and I'm close to collapse."

Tawny Owl, Kestrel and the pheasants flew on ahead and perched on the railings surrounding the army area. Fox lined up the animals at the edge of the road. There was no traffic, but dawn was breaking. Soon people would be astir. Each of the larger animals took charge of a group of youngsters and ferried them over. Then Weasel ran with the voles and mice. Soon all the animals except Toad had crossed. They squeezed through the railings and hid themselves in a gorse thicket. Many of them fell asleep at once. Fox stood aside, watching them all settle. Suddenly he became aware that Toad wasn't amongst them.

"Where's Toad?" he muttered.

Pheasant called out, "He hasn't crossed. I don't think he can make it."

In a trice Fox dashed back to the road. Toad was squatting forlornly on the other side. Fox ran over.

"I'm just … taking a … breather," Toad explained weakly.

"No time for that," Fox snapped. He could see the lights of an approaching car. "Quickly, grasp my tail and climb up!" He felt Toad's grip. As soon as he was sure Toad was off the ground he raced away. He just regained the other side as the car swept by. Fox and Toad rejoined the others. Moments later they were sound asleep.

Throughout the next day everyone slept, save for Kestrel and the two pheasants. In the evening, Mole woke first. He felt famished and went in search of worms. Here, as everywhere, the ground was baked hard by the drought. Mole found digging difficult.

"There's a better place than that for digging," Kestrel's voice screeched from nearby.

Mole looked up. Kestrel was peering down from a holly branch. "There's marshy land nearby," the bird continued. "Soft and wet soil. Ideal for worm-gathering."

"I'm most grateful," said Mole. "Can you show me where?"

Kestrel pointed her wing and Mole set off eagerly.

When the others awoke it was evening but still light.

Food was the priority for each animal. All of them went in search of their requirements. Only Toad, who was still tired, stayed put. Badger made a mental note to bring him back some worms.

On their return, Fox decided they should rest a few more hours before continuing with their journey. Because of Toad's fatigue Fox knew that in future they must travel in shorter stages. The animals and the day-flying birds napped whilst Tawny Owl kept watch. When Owl thought they had slept long enough she woke Fox.

"I think we should press on," said the bird. "Make use of the darkness."

"You're quite right," Fox agreed. "We can take a drink at the marsh first and refresh ourselves. Toad should have recovered by then." He gently woke his companions and the group made for the marsh. Adder stayed with Toad.

Mole, hanging on to Badger's fur as before, hoped for an opportunity to dig for some more worms. He seemed to be permanently hungry. He mentioned his idea to Badger.

"No, Mole, you won't have time," said the old creature. "We have to move on."

But when the animals were all drinking from the dark marshy water, Mole made off while their backs were turned. "Just a few juicy mouthfuls, then I'll go straight back," he told himself. Unfortunately he had strayed too far from dry land and, as he dug, water began to seep into the hole.

The animals finished drinking. Fox requested Hare, as the swiftest runner, to go back and tell Toad and Adder to join them.

"Are we all ready to go on?" Fox asked as they all waited.

Badger looked round for Mole to tell him to take his usual place. Of course Mole was absent. Badger guessed at once what had happened.

"He's so greedy," he said crossly. "I'm afraid he's hidden himself somewhere." He went to look for signs of

Mole's digging. He soon found the hole, which was now full of water. Badger was alarmed and hastened to tell Fox.

"My goodness!" Fox exclaimed. "We'd better dig him out before he drowns." But as fast as they dug in the spongy soil, the faster the hole gathered more water.

"It appears we're too late," Fox said grimly. "He must have drowned already."

"Oh, Mole!" Badger cried. "What have you done?"

"We'll try another hole," Fox suggested. "Just in case he —" He broke off. Hare's voice was calling them urgently.

"What's that?" Badger asked.

"Sssh," Fox hissed. "Listen!"

Hare bounded towards them. "Fire!" he yelled. "Run for your lives! FIRE!"

The Search for Mole

The animals panicked. Even Fox quailed at the news. A red glow could be seen amongst the distant trees. Mole was forgotten. Fox steeled himself.

"Hare!" he cried. "Where are Toad and Adder?"

"They're in the path of the flames," Hare panted. "They're coming as fast as they can but — "

"Toad'll never save himself," Fox gasped. "I'm going back for him. Badger, I'm leaving you in charge. Take the party round to the other side of the marsh. The damp ground may check the fire's advance." He galloped away towards the lurid red glow.

"Right, everybody, come with me," Badger ordered. "Owl, wait here and look for Adder. She should be coming soon."

Treading carefully to avoid sinking into the marsh itself, the animals slowly skirted the water. They reached slightly higher ground. From here they could look back over the marsh and see the movement of the flames.

"Father, will we ever see Fox again?" one of the leverets asked Hare.

"Of course we will," he answered. "He'll be back. You'll see."

Fox sped back towards the gorse thicket, trying to quell his own fear. He had to find Toad. Without him to point the way, they were all stranded. The fire grew brighter as Fox approached it. The air felt hot and scorched. Fox heard the crackle of the flames. "Toad! Toad! Are you there?" he called. As he neared the blaze his courage almost failed him. He could barely stand the intense heat. He paused. He felt he could go no further. He heard a desperate croak.

"Fox! Have you come back for me? Here I am." Toad crawled out from some undergrowth.

"Thank goodness! Hasten, Toad! The flames will be on us in a moment." Even as he spoke, the fire burst upon them with a mighty roar. Toad made a huge leap forward. Fox bent and gently took the little creature in his jaws. He turned and galloped away. They heard sirens in the distance, traffic and human voices. Fox halted only once to allow Toad to climb on his back. Then he pelted towards the marsh.

While his friends fled for their lives, Mole, deep underground, had remained ignorant of the fire. Worms were plentiful and he had a feast. Eventually he felt his feet and fur were wet and he realized the hole was filling up with water. He couldn't climb directly upwards so he dug forward, intending to surface at another spot. Then he began to dig his way up. He grew hotter and hotter. The soil felt hot, too, almost burning him. He slipped back a little. He was trapped between the fire and the water.

Tawny Owl had waited patiently for Adder. The snake shot through the dry grass, desperate to keep ahead of the flames. As soon as Owl spied her rippling body, she called directions. "Round the marsh, Adder! The other side of the water!" Then she flew in search of Fox.

Fox, running at breakneck speed, saw the ghostly grey shape of the bird lit by the light of the fire. "It's all right, Owl," he called. "We're coming. Take cover yourself."

Soon the three of them had joined the rest of the throng. Badger said mournfully, "Poor Mole's journey is ended."

Mole, however, was still alive and bitterly regretting his greediness. "Oh, Badger. Oh, Fox! I wish you could help me. If I ever get out of here I'll never stray again. Oh dear!" He sobbed in his fright and finally cried himself to sleep.

He was wakened by the vibrations of heavy footsteps overhead. He knew these were not animal feet. The crashing above told him humans were about. He shuddered at this fresh danger.

Gradually the din passed over. The noise became fainter. Mole began carefully to inch upwards. The soil had cooled. He smelt the burnt land above. He wriggled to the surface. It was daylight. Everything around was black. There seemed to be no life anywhere. The earth was wet and still smoked in places. Mole knew there had been a terrible fire and

that the humans had come with water to quench it. He felt certain all his friends had perished.

"Oh, I wish I were dead, too!" he howled. "Where can I go on my own?" He lay down, his head on his paws, and wept bitterly for Badger and Fox and all the animals.

Fox had kept the animals out of sight while they watched the firemen with their huge machines douse the flames. As the men prepared to leave Toad said,

"All this destruction from one human's carelessness. A cigarette thrown from a car! How many creatures have died because of human thoughtlessness?"

Badger was reminded of Mole and felt very sad. "I don't suppose, Fox, I could have one last look for Mole? Just in case he survived?"

Fox looked doubtful. "Is it likely, Badger? The whole area is ruined. I think we should get away from this horrible place now."

Badger looked so sorrowful that Fox relented. "All right, then. Your kindness does you credit. But don't spend too long."

The men had moved off. Badger ran back to where he'd last seen Mole. It didn't take him long to discover the little animal lying on the surface. Mole's twitching nose told Badger he was alive.

"Oh, this is wonderful!" Badger cried. Mole was soon up on the old creature's back again, almost before he had realized what had happened. On the way they told each other of their experiences.

Then Mole said, "It's the second time you've rescued me and I promise, Badger, greed will never get the better of me again."

The Animals are Trapped

Mole was overjoyed to see all his friends. As they set off again, a distinct change occurred in the weather. Dark clouds rolled up, blotting out the sun. Moments later the first drops of rain began to fall. The animals rejoiced to feel the first rain for weeks on their bodies. The rain grew heavier. There were flashes of lightning and thunderclaps. The animals were soon drenched. Only Toad continued to enjoy the rainfall. He loved water and he croaked a tune to keep their spirits up.

"This is most unfortunate," said Badger. "After the ordeal of the fire, now we have to endure a storm."

Toad led them out of the army land into farming country. The open fields provided no shelter at all and the voles and fieldmice were thoroughly miserable.

"I seem to remember a shed hereabouts," Toad remarked. "I'll keep my eyes open for it."

"You could hardly find it with them closed," Adder drawled.

They entered an orchard of pear and plum trees. At the far end of it was a long, low wooden building.

"That's it!" Toad cried. "I'm sure of it."

Tawny Owl flew on ahead, eager to find a roost. She didn't relish flying in the daylight and felt sleepy. She found the shed door open and fluttered in.

The animals trooped inside, relieved to find somewhere dry to settle. There was straw on the floor and some empty boxes. It was a fruit store. Fox watched the animals making temporary nests. He wondered if the open door meant someone was planning to return. He sent Kestrel to keep watch from a fruit tree and told Pheasant to relieve her later.

All the party made themselves comfortable. They nestled up together on the floor, but were careful to avoid the hedgehogs.

"This is marvellous," said a hedgehog. "We're so snug we'll be dry in no time." He had rolled himself up in the straw.

Tawny Owl perched on an empty shelf, her head under her wing. Adder coiled herself up and watched the mice with a wicked grin. No one wanted to sleep near the snake.

When Kestrel's watch was over she flew to the shed. Her feathers were quite dry. The storm had long since died down. She saw everyone was asleep. She nudged Pheasant. "You and your mate must go and watch now," she said. "The safety of the party is in your care."

Tom Griggs, the farmer, owned the surrounding land. He was in a black mood. His crops were being ruined by the weather and he had lost four of his chickens to a fox. He longed to catch the culprit. After the storm he took up his shotgun and stumped around the fields to survey the damage. As he trudged unhappily back through his small orchard the cock pheasant rose up from the long grass. Griggs put the gun to his shoulder and fired clean through it. The bird crumpled and fell to earth. The sound of the shot scared Pheasant's mate. She also took to the air and Griggs shot her, too. A brace of pheasant to take home was some consolation for what the farmer had lost.

As he neared his cottage his wife called to him. Griggs held the birds aloft in triumph. "You come and see what I've found," she called. She was standing by the fruit store with their dog, Jack. The shed door was closed. Griggs peered through the shed window.

"It's – it's full of animals," he gasped.

"Including your fox!" exclaimed Mrs Griggs. "They must have run in there from the storm. Did you ever see such a thing?"

"Have you shut the door tight?" the farmer grunted.

"Good and tight."

"That fox won't escape me this time," growled Griggs. "Now, Jack, you sit there and guard the creatures properly. I'm going inside to clean and re-load my gun. Then I'm going to settle a score or two."

The animals had woken when the door was slammed shut. They soon saw they might be trapped. The windows were tightly closed. They ran about, looking for a crevice or a crack in the woodwork which they could crawl through. Whilst they were searching they heard the gunfire outside and the alarm call of a pheasant. Then a second shot.

"The pheasants are done for," Adder said bluntly.

Fox tried to calm the animals. "Quiet, everyone! Let me think." He paced up and down the shed. "Now I know we're in danger, but there must be a way out."

"There's only one way out," Tawny Owl commented. "Dig!"

"Of course!" Fox cried. "We'll dig ourselves out."

Human voices outside made them freeze. When the farmer and his wife had gone Fox asked, "Who's our best tunneller?"

"Mole," Badger replied at once.

Mole swelled with pride. At last he could be of use.

Then he looked at the floor. "Oh! I can't dig through that," he wailed. He scratched at the wooden floor. He was close to tears.

"Leave that to us," said the squirrels. "We can gnaw."

"So can we," said the voles and mice.

Their powerful teeth soon got to work on the floor, scraping, biting and rasping. They made such a din that the farm dog outside began to growl. Adder slid to the gap under the door where, by hissing and lunging, she kept the dog at bay.

The thin planks of wood soon gave way before the animals' powerful teeth. Once the hole was big enough Mole squeezed through and began to dig downwards. When he was able to, Badger followed him and helped him to make the tunnel bigger so that all the animals could use it. The two worked hard and dug along under the shed until they were clear of it and could pull themselves out in the orchard.

"Free again!" Mole sang happily.

Badger called to Fox. "It's ready! We've dug to the orchard."

Fox stood in the shed, overseeing the group of animals. One by one they went through the hole in the floor into the tunnel. Adder kept the dog occupied so that it suspected nothing.

"I can see the farmer coming," she warned Fox. "And he has his gun."

Fox was last into the hole, then Adder slipped in behind him. Soon all the animals were safely into the orchard. The birds had walked through the tunnel and were very glad to be in the open air again where they could use their wings.

Meanwhile Griggs flung the door open to find a shed empty except for a large pile of earth on the floor. The dog bounded inside.

"You stupid beast!" Griggs cursed the animal. "You've let them get away!"

Clever Fox

Toad lost no time in leading the animals away from the farmland into open country. They arrived at the foot of a hill, and paused briefly.

"We're very exposed here," Fox remarked. "Do we have to go up that hill?"

"Oh yes," said Toad. "I remember it clearly. On the other side is a dense copse where we can stop and rest."

"There's no one about," Kestrel screeched from the air. "You should keep going now and get under cover."

The smaller animals were very weary but they didn't like being in the open. They hastened on to the slope. The party continued onwards, not realizing that Jack, the farmer's dog, had picked up their scent and was following their trail. Kestrel and Tawny Owl called encouragement from the top of the rise as the animals struggled on. About halfway up Fox thought he heard a distant bark. He ignored it. But Kestrel's piercing gaze had picked out Jack running on their track. "Make haste!" she cried. "You're being pursued."

Fox halted. He heard another, louder bark. "I'll deal with this," he said grimly. "Badger, look after the others. Take them to the copse."

"Look after *yourself*," Toad shouted behind him as Fox stood his ground.

Fox could see the dog at the bottom of the slope. "Here I am!" he called. "I'm the one you're after; forget the rest."

"Yes, you're the one," the dog growled and began to pound uphill. "My master ... wants you ... dead." The dog paused a few metres away. "You killed his chickens," he panted. "He wants his revenge."

"I never killed a chicken in my life," Fox replied calmly. "You've got the wrong beast."

"A likely story," Jack growled. "Why were you on my master's land?"

"We took shelter from the storm," said Fox. "That's all. Then we were trapped."

"I don't believe you," Jack said. "I'm taking you back."

"You'll have to kill me first. That won't please your master who I'm quite sure is already angry with you."

The dog wavered.

"You see," Fox went on, "your master wants to do the

killing. And, besides, the fox who killed the chickens is still loose so why aren't you hunting *him?*"

"Oh, you're so clever," the dog barked. But he was beaten and Fox knew it. Fox turned on his heel and coolly walked away, leaving the dog gaping after him. He disappeared over the brow of the hill and broke into a run as Jack, the farm dog, slunk homewards.

Fox's friends were full of praise for the way he had sent the dog packing. They entered the copse together. The tall trees and undergrowth gave them a feeling of security. The animals and birds went at once to search for food. Afterwards they found comfortable places to rest in.

"We'll spend some time here," Fox decided. "There's no danger of interference and it will give us a chance to regain our strength. We've come a long way."

Toad shook his head. "There's more of the journey ahead than behind us. We've more farmland to cross, then meadows, then a river, then ..."

"All right, Toad," Fox interrupted. "That'll do for now. When we've had a few quiet days here we'll be ready for the challenge."

So the party relaxed and enjoyed their brief stay under the shade of the tall trees. About a week later Fox decided it was time to move on. He gathered everyone together and, at dusk, they left the copse.

Travelling by night and resting under cover by day, the party neared the river. This arrangement didn't suit everyone. Many of the animals were normally active during daylight. Kestrel in particular hated flying in the dark. But it was the safest way to travel and avoided humans as much as possible. After several days Toad brought them to the bank of the river.

"It looks daunting," said Weasel.

"No, no, nothing to it," replied Toad who was an excellent swimmer.

"Well, it's a long swim for mice," said a fieldmouse.

"Don't worry," said Toad. "I'll go across first. You watch me. I'm your sort of size and, if I can do it ..." He leapt into the water and kicked out for the far shore. Minutes later they heard his croaks of triumph from the opposite bank. "I've made it! Come and join me!"

Kestrel and Tawny Owl flew over and perched by Toad's side.

"Line up along the bank, everyone," said Fox. "We'll all go together."

The mice and voles collected in the middle, flanked

by the squirrels and hedgehogs. The rabbits, Hare and his family and Badger were on the far right; Weasel, Fox, Mole and Adder on the far left. Fox and Badger stepped down to the water and the smaller animals kept level. They began to swim.

Mole and Badger, both good swimmers, were soon ahead of the rest. The hares and hedgehogs and Adder were behind them. Fox and Weasel swam more slowly, trying to keep an eye on the more nervous members of the party. The voles and fieldmice, though tiny, stuck to the task. Only the squirrels and rabbits took fright. Weasel calmed the squirrels and Fox tried to steady the rabbits who were beginning to panic. In little bunches, the animals reached the far bank. With relief they pulled their dripping bodies on to dry land again. At last the squirrels arrived with Weasel and then only the rabbits were missing from the group. They had paid no attention to Fox's advice and were swimming round and round in circles, thrashing the water in their alarm. Fox paddled from one rabbit to another, vainly trying to steer it in the right direction. His struggles came to nothing and he began to tire.

"He needs help," said Badger. "And without delay." Upstream he had noticed a huge mass of debris, made up of leaves, grass, twigs and even small branches, bearing down on Fox and the rabbits. "They're in danger," Badger cried. "Everyone who can must rescue one rabbit. I'll look after Fox. Be quick — lives are at stake!"

The strongest swimmers singled out a rabbit each and, in various ways, pushed or tugged them to safety. Then Fox and Badger were alone in the river. Fox had exhausted himself trying to help the rabbits and could only manage a feeble paddle. Badger refused to desert him. Fox saw that the massed debris was almost upon them. "Badger, please leave me," he begged. "Save yourself."

Badger ignored him, still trying to keep Fox afloat. He steeled himself for the sudden collision. Voices of alarm and distress reached Badger from the bank. Then he was struck heavily on his side and pulled underwater. Fox caught a blow from a branch and was carried away downstream, but Badger had completely disappeared.

Fox is Swept Away

The throng of animals watched these events with horror. As Fox was swept away they raced along the bank, trying to keep him in sight. He was soon lost from view. However the birds continued to follow him, flying along the course of the river. Downstream the water flowed more swiftly and at one point there was a large rock in the river. Here the debris broke into two pieces, the half carrying Fox rushing past on one side and the other half becoming lodged against the rock.

"Look!" cried Toad, pointing to the mass of trapped vegetation. "There's something moving there. It's …"

"It's Badger!" Mole finished for him in great excitement.

Sure enough, amongst the swirling weed, they could see Badger's striped face.

"Come on, we must get him out," said Weasel. She and Hare and a few of the hedgehogs jumped once more into the water. Using all their strength they managed to reach the rock. Between them they clawed Badger free and pushed and nudged his limp body back to the bank. The old animal was in a very poor state. His eyes were closed, his coat filthy, and his sides heaved violently as he fought for breath. To the joy of all he slowly began to recover.

The rabbits stood shamefaced as Badger heaved himself clear of the water. They knew they were to blame for the disaster. The animals milled around, uncertain what to do now that they were leaderless.

Badger stumbled to some undergrowth and sank down, his head on his paws. He was completely spent.

The others surrounded him. The rabbits mumbled apologies for their stupidity.

"That won't bring Fox back," Weasel said savagely.

A while later Tawny Owl arrived back. "Kestrel flies faster and her eyesight's keener," she explained. "She'll keep up with Fox."

"Meanwhile," Toad said, "we need a new leader."

"But we can't go on without Fox," said Mole.

"Of course we can. We must. What else can we do?" demanded Tawny Owl.

"If Fox survives he'll catch us up," said Weasel. "That's all any of us can hope for."

"Well, who's to be this new leader?" asked Hare.

"Badger, who else?" Mole answered.

"Is he in a fit state?" Tawny Owl wondered.

"He soon will be," said Weasel. "We'll leave him alone now. He needs a long rest."

Hours passed. The animals found food for themselves and Badger and fell asleep around him. At dawn the next day they awoke to find Kestrel had returned.

"It's bad news," she told them. "I followed Fox a long way – as far as a bridge over the river. Fox was alive when he went under it but he didn't come out the other side. I waited and waited but – nothing. I don't know what happened. There was a small boat going under the bridge. Perhaps Fox hit it."

There was a stunned silence. None of them could quite believe Fox was dead. Badger broke the silence.

"We'll move on tonight," he announced. "The journey continues. Do you hear me, everyone? Be ready to leave tonight."

The party was happy to accept Badger's authority. But they were heavy-hearted at the loss of the brave and clever Fox. Mole felt awkward about Badger's continuing to carry him after nearly drowning in the river.

"It's all right, Mole," Badger said kindly. "I'm fully recovered. And we must try and keep hopeful, all of us. Fox may even now be making his way back to us."

"Hardly likely if he hit a boat," Adder muttered.

Toad took them through meadows on to wide, open downland. The night breezes and the springy grass raised their spirits. Farthing Wood was far enough behind them to be missed no longer. They felt confident that, with or without Fox, they would reach their goal, the Nature Reserve.

Unknown to his friends, Fox was very much alive. The branch sweeping him downriver had taken him under the bridge as Kestrel had seen. There it had caught against the outboard motor of a small boat. The man in the boat was quite unaware he was trailing a fox along. Fox raised himself, wondering whether to risk a jump into the boat itself. Up ahead the river broadened. The man steered his craft towards the bank. He intended to moor and do a spot of fishing. Fox saw his chance. As the bank neared he scrambled astern the boat and, with a great leap, landed ashore. The man cried out in astonishment. People walking on the tow-path stopped to watch. Their mouths dropped open as Fox dashed between their legs and raced for the nearest field.

He could think of nothing except finding his way back to his friends. He knew the river was the key to this. He must keep it in sight and try to work his way back to where the disaster had happened. He longed to know Badger's fate and whether all the others had got safely out of the water.

An ancient black horse stood in the field, watching Fox. As Fox came up the horse said, "You're a bold one, running about in the daylight. This is all hunting country round here."

Fox stopped running. The warning was timely. "I'm grateful to you," he said. "I'll be doubly careful. I've never been involved with the Hunt and I don't want to start now."

"I wish you luck," the horse wheezed as Fox loped away.

Fox ran on, looking for signs of his friends. He was puzzled that none of them had come in search of him. He realized they might think he had drowned. Had they continued the journey without him? If so, they could be much farther ahead. He increased his pace. Ravenous as he was, he didn't pause to eat. He had a lot of ground to cover.

Towards evening he knew he must rest for a few hours and refresh himself. He returned to the river's edge to drink; then he snapped up some worms and insects to stave off his hunger. He found a place to sleep under a weeping willow. He felt terribly alone.

Fox meets Vixen

During the night Fox awoke and set off again. He ran through the dark hours, snatching a morsel here and there. Dawn approached. He was very weary. He had tired himself out and he looked around for somewhere safe to rest. In a corner of one field, under a hedgerow, he discovered a large burrow. It seemed ideal and he crept inside. It was empty and he soon fell asleep.

Fox awoke with a start as something touched his body. There was a strong scent of female fox. He jumped up.

"Don't be alarmed," said the vixen. "Stay and rest. I must go in search of food."

"I'm sorry I intruded," said Fox.

"Don't be. This is only one of my retreats. I haven't seen you before. Have you been travelling?"

"Travelling?" Fox smiled. "Yes. It's a long story."

"I'd like to hear it," said Vixen. "But food comes first. Will you join me?"

"At once. I'm famished."

The two animals hunted prey together. Fox was struck by Vixen's beauty. She was the most wonderful creature he had ever seen. They slipped back to the earth with their catch which they devoured between them in silence.

Afterwards Fox began his tale. He told Vixen about the destruction of Farthing Wood and how he and his friends were travelling across country to a new home in White Deer Park. He told her of the river crossing and how he had been separated from the party and was now hastening to rejoin it.

"How brave you all are," Vixen murmured.

"Tell me about yourself," said Fox.

"Oh, there's nothing to tell," she replied. "I haven't lost *my* home to the humans, although I've had my brushes with them."

"The Hunt?" Fox whispered.

She nodded.

"Why stay in this area? If you were my mate you'd have nothing to fear. You could travel with me to find my friends and I would protect you. We could make a new home together."

Vixen's eyes shone. She was flattered. "I will travel with you until you find your friends," was all she would promise.

Fox understood. He had to prove himself.

When Vixen had rested, the pair of foxes left her earth and made for the riverside. Some while later they reached the place where the Farthing Wood party had swum the river. Fox began to search for a clue as to the direction his friends had taken. He first found a patch of flattened grass where the animals had slept. From there he was able to pick up their trail.

"This is it," he said to Vixen excitedly. "I can smell Badger's scent. Thank heaven he's alive!" He galloped forward.

"What a surprise they will have," said Vixen, "when they see you again."

"A double surprise when they see my companion," Fox added joyfully.

When they reached the downland Vixen paused. This was new territory and she couldn't decide whether to leave her familiar range.

"What's wrong?" Fox asked.

"Why don't you go on and find your friends? They may not want a stranger amongst them. If they have no objection you can come back and fetch me."

Fox nodded. "You want time to think," he said. "Very well. But, Vixen, I shall be in turmoil until I know your decision."

"I'll give you my answer when you return."

The Farthing Wood party were not far in advance of Fox. It was morning and they were climbing a steep slope which led up to a small spinney. As they neared the top they heard the distant sound of human shouts. Dogs barked and horses' hooves thudded. The animals hesitated. The noise approached swiftly. Soon they were in no doubt that they were listening to the sound dreaded by wild creatures everywhere. The sound of the Hunt. They hurried on. On the level ground to their left they saw the eager hounds. They saw the horses carrying scarlet- and black-coated riders. The hounds had not yet found a scent.

"Let us hope no foxes are about today," said Toad. He knew the same thought was in all the animals' minds.

They reached the clump of trees at the summit, thankful to hide themselves away. Suddenly a startling new cry was carried on the breeze. The hounds were baying with excitement. The friends rushed in a mass to the edge of the slope and peered down. Now the hounds were at full-tilt over the downland with the horses galloping behind them.

"They've picked up a scent," Tawny Owl said grimly. "Some poor creature's got the race of his life ahead of him."

Vixen had not spent long coming to a decision. When Fox had left her she soon realized she did wish to stay with him. He would make an ideal mate and she knew she was lucky to have met him. She thought she wouldn't wait for his return but run to catch him up. She took a short cut through a wood. She expected to be ahead of him when she came out the other side. Halfway through the wood she heard the hounds. Whose trail were they on?

She listened. The Hunt was coming nearer … nearer … nearer … It was hers! The dogs crashed into the wood, yelling furiously. Vixen's heart raced. She spurted away towards a thick screen of brambles and ferns. She thought she could entangle the hounds in its mass while she made good her escape. The dogs followed her, gaining on her. But once she was in the undergrowth, her lighter, more supple body began to leave them behind. A little further and she would be out of the wood, on the open downland and free. Yet, even as she pulled herself out of the last of the tearing brambles, she saw the cunning of humans. The horsemen had reined in their mounts. They were outside the wood at the very point where Vixen would emerge from it. Many of the hounds were thronging there, ready to ambush her. She saw their blazing eyes and snapping teeth. The game was up.

The Hunt

When the first yelps of the pack reached him, Fox stopped dead. The horrible sound made his blood run cold. Where were his friends? Could he rejoin them before the Hunt barred his way? It soon became clear that he was not the quarry the hounds sought. They followed another trail. Fox felt intense relief. Another poor creature was the hunted one. He would soon be with his friends again. He ran on. But the thought of Vixen made him halt again. Suppose his lovely new companion was the victim? He knew at once he must find out. He couldn't abandon her to her fate.

He changed course and ran towards the sounds of the Hunt. He saw the wood and the dogs plunging into it. He saw the huntsmen coolly waiting outside it. Fox knew their quarry was nearby. He raced towards them.

Confusion broke out amongst them. They had not expected a second fox on the scene and even the hounds were at a loss. Here was a fox actually running towards them!

Fox dashed through the group. He felt fresh and strong. He pelted away from them and the confused animals didn't at once follow him. This gave him a good start. He went at breakneck speed across the grass towards a steep rise in the land. Vixen had witnessed Fox's heroic action and now she scrambled free from the undergrowth. So the hounds were split into two packs, each chasing different animals.

Fox had made a grave mistake in running for the slope. It was steep and a little way up he began to tire. The hounds steadily closed the gap. He heard their harsh pants of breath. Then, as if in a dream, he heard well-loved voices calling to him from the top of the slope. Badger, Mole, Tawny Owl, Weasel, Toad and all the others had been watching the moves of the Hunt in unbearable tension. They hadn't realized until now that the poor pursued animal was their own beloved Fox. Their cries urged him on. He reached the top and staggered into the welcoming circle of his old friends. At once they hustled him into the spinney. They surrounded him, prepared to fight to the death against the hounds.

The Hunt was close, almost at the brow of the hill. The huntsman's horn blew. Amazingly, the Hunt swerved, abruptly taking a different course. Kestrel

flew out of the spinney to watch events. Fox guessed what had happened.

"It's Vixen," he panted. "They've given up on me. She's still in the open and easier to chase. I thought I'd saved her!" He mumbled a short explanation of how he and Vixen had met and travelled together.

The stunned animals didn't know what to say. Kestrel returned and urged them to escape. "Our way is clear," she said. "Another fox is the quarry. We can all profit by it."

Badger told her the news. "Even if *we* leave here," he finished by saying, "Fox would never come with us. He's lost his heart to this Vixen."

Fox's agony was shared by his friends. They had to see the outcome. Vixen was nearer than they had expected. She was running in their direction in a last pitiful effort to find Fox. She looked up and saw him.

She was exhausted but somehow her legs kept moving. Fox spurred her on and the hounds actually lost ground. But the Master of the Hunt wasn't of a mind to let a second fox escape. He galloped up behind Vixen. He raised his whip-handle, his arm poised for the blow that would knock her down.

Suddenly in the grass under his horse's feet a snake lifted its head. It lunged forward, burying its fangs in the horse's foreleg. The horse screamed in pain. It reared, throwing its cruel rider to earth with a dull thud. He lay still.

In the next second, Vixen reached Fox and the entire party retreated under the trees. The hounds were called off as the other riders dismounted to help the injured man. Adder had put paid to the day's hunting.

Behind the screen of trees the animals watched the Hunt depart. Adder was greeted as a heroine but all she said was, "What else could I do? I was about to be trampled."

They all wanted to celebrate. The party was reunited and they had a charming new companion in Vixen. The foxes exchanged fond glances. Then Fox said, "We've an awful lot to tell each other, but now's not the time. We should move to a safer place."

The animals didn't linger. They followed Toad towards a disused gravel pit which was enclosed and therefore a perfect place to rest. They dug their way under the fence and hid themselves amongst the wild plants.

Fox and Vixen told their tale and heard the others' news. A warm glow of companionship bathed them all. When Toad told them there wasn't much farther to travel they fell asleep contented and happy.

The Journey Continues

They were wakened the next morning by a strange whistling sound. A heron stood close by, slowly flapping his grey wings. One wing had been punctured by a shotgun pellet. The air rushing through this hole produced the whistle. The animals watched him curiously.

"Good morning," said the tall bird. "I've been hoping to meet you. I know all about your feats and adventures. Word travels fast in the bird world. I'm known as Whistler. You can guess the reason."

"What can we do for you?" Badger asked.

"Nothing really, except allow me to travel with you," the heron answered. "Life can be very lonely when you're by yourself. I often fish here in the pond you see down there. Plenty of fish but — alas! — no company. I'm wondering if there might be an interesting female heron in your Nature Reserve."

Fox, who knew all about the pleasures of finding a mate, made the heron welcome. "The more the merrier," he said. He didn't know then that Whistler would more than prove his worth on the journey to come.

That evening the friends left the gravel-pit with their two new and charming companions. For the next few weeks they continued their way across the downland. At the end of it, Toad told them there would be a wide road to cross. It was the last major obstacle before White Deer Park.

"I don't think it'll be much of a hazard," Toad had said. "When I passed this way before the humans hadn't finished building it. If we're careful we should be able to avoid them."

One day the end of the downland was in sight. The sound of motor traffic had recently become very noticeable and Fox was concerned. It was daylight.

"Kestrel, will you go on ahead and explore?" he asked the keen-eyed bird.

Kestrel returned with disturbing news. "Toad's new road has been completed," she told them. "There are six lanes of traffic on it with a sort of refuge in the middle. It's frighteningly busy. I don't know how you animals will cope."

Toad looked crestfallen. "I-I'm sorry," he mumbled.

"Not your fault," Fox answered. "We all know to our cost how fast humans can work."

"What can we do?" wailed a squirrel.

"Cross it, of course," Adder lisped. "White Deer Park won't come to us."

"We'll all be killed," a rabbit muttered nervously.

The animals grimly continued on to a line of trees. The motorway was beyond that. Kestrel flew up high to watch developments. She called excitedly from the air, "The traffic's stuck fast on one side! If you move quickly you can get across to the halfway point now."

The animals ran to the bank above the road. The noise and smell of the traffic was frightful. Cars and lorries of all sizes were stationary on the near side. Their exhaust fumes choked the still air. Separating

these vehicles from those roaring past in the opposite
direction was the central reservation, a narrow strip of
grass and weeds within crash barriers.

Fox took the situation in at a glance. "We mustn't
hesitate," he told the party. "We must run to the middle
before these machines start moving again."

Whistler took him at his word and flew to the centre
where he awaited the others. Vixen shepherded the
mice and voles in front of her. Fox took charge of the
squirrels and hedgehogs. They threaded their way
through the unmoving traffic, under bumpers and
between wheels, and arrived at the refuge. Weasel,
Hare and his family and the rabbits were behind them.
They wrinkled their noses in disgust at the fumes. Then

Badger and Mole and Toad brought up the rear. Adder had fallen behind. Tawny Owl and Kestrel went to look for her.

The Farthing Wood animals mingled in the centre of the motorway. Astonished human faces gazed at them from inside the vehicles. Children's noses were pressed to the glass. Their arms waved in bewilderment. But the animals were safe from interference. They watched for a gap in the speeding traffic on the other side.

"There must come a lull sooner or later," said Fox.

"I think I may be of some use here," Whistler offered. "I could carry some of the smaller animals across in my long beak."

"A wonderful idea!" exclaimed Fox.

"I can begin right away," the heron said. "I'll deposit the youngsters on the opposite bank."

"Right. Hare, Rabbits, get the little ones ready."

Whistler bent and, with extreme gentleness, picked up the first youngster and ferried him to the far bank. One by one he carried them across. Then he gave lifts to the voles and fieldmice. These were easy. Toad was no weight either. Weasel and the squirrels were dealt with in a similar way. Then Whistler confessed himself beaten.

The number of animals in the centre had dwindled dramatically. Many were now safely across the entire road thanks to the heroic Whistler. At that point the stationary vehicles began to move again. The animals halfway across were trapped between two flows of traffic. They waited impatiently for their opportunity. At last they saw a chance. The adult hares, the swiftest runners, sprinted over during the first lull. Next Fox and Vixen and the adult rabbits ran across. Badger, carrying Mole, and the hedgehogs were slower. They had to wait for a wider gap in the traffic. Tawny Owl and Kestrel flew to join their friends on the far bank. Adder had been sighted but there was now no way she could cross any part of the motorway.

"Ready, Mole. We can run soon," said Badger as he saw the last car in a group approach. "Ready, hedgehogs!"

They lumbered across and Badger and most of the hedgehogs reached safety. But two older hedgehogs were very slow. As the next bunch of vehicles neared they instinctively rolled themselves up into balls. This was the very worst thing they could have done. Poor hedgehogs, it was all over in a trice. Their friends on the bank watched dumbly. No one spoke for several minutes. Then Vixen said, "We're lucky no more lives were lost."

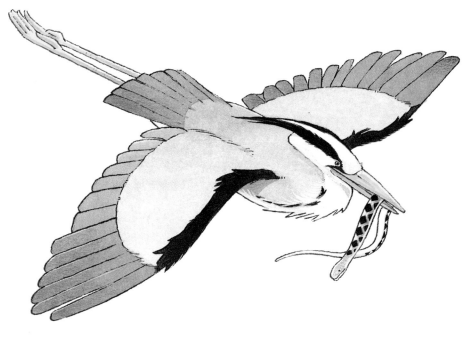

A New Home at Last

Fox led the saddened animals down the bank into a cornfield. They tried to forget the horror of the motorway. Whistler remained on the ridge. He kept a look-out for Adder on the other side of the road. When the heron saw the snake's scaly body wriggling through the grass he flew over. He snatched up the startled snake in his beak.

"This is most undignified," she protested.

Whistler ignored her and the Farthing Wood animals cheered up when they saw the heron flying towards them. Adder looked so comical dangling from his beak like a gigantic earthworm.

The cornfield became the animals' resting-place for the rest of the day. Toad was in high spirits. He knew that the long journey was almost over. He looked forward to leading the animals into the Nature Reserve. All serious danger was behind them. They would soon be on the final lap.

That night the animals moved off again. Toad's enthusiasm had made them all light-hearted. But they kept their usual caution.

"We'll soon be there, we'll soon be there," the youngsters chanted.

"We mustn't relax our guard," Fox warned. "The human presence is everywhere. We can't afford to slip up now."

"Haven't there been slips already?" a hedgehog asked pointedly.

"There had to be some losses," Tawny Owl remarked. "It's unfortunate but unavoidable."

"Easy to say when you're not affected," said the hedgehog.

"We're all affected," said Badger. "We're all friends and the loss of a friend is felt by everyone."

"We've come through an awful lot together," said Fox. "How many of us actually thought we'd still be together after such a long time?"

"And almost within sight of White Deer Park," Toad added.

"Is it really that close?" Mole asked

"One more day's travel," replied Toad, "and we'll be within the Nature Reserve."

There was silence as each creature or family thought

about the new life they would make for themselves.

"I shall eat a huge meal and then sleep for days," Tawny Owl said. "I've had more than my fair share of sleeping and waking at the wrong times."

"Same here," said Kestrel. "I shall never have to fly by night again."

"I shall look round at once for a suitable site for my new set," said Badger. "It'll be wonderful to be able to sleep underground again."

"Yes, there's nothing like an underground home," Mole agreed. "I shall dig the finest network of tunnels a mole could have."

"I'm looking forward to living a normal life up a tree," said a squirrel.

"To be able to run free with my family where *I* choose is my dream," Hare confessed.

"To be able to nibble at leisure," said a rabbit.

"To swim when I want to!" cried Toad.

"To go foraging in the moonlight," said Weasel.

"To meet someone of one's own kind again," sighed Whistler.

The animals looked at Fox. "What about you?" they asked him.

Fox looked proudly at Vixen. "There's my answer." He smiled. Vixen smiled back. "To be," Fox said, "safe from interference in our new home."

"And," Adder lisped, "for this everlasting trek to come to an end."

The animals laughed heartily. They felt content and

warm in one another's company.

The animals needed one more resting-place. They found it under a hedgerow and gladly lay down together. Dawn was breaking and Kestrel decided to fly on and find White Deer Park.

Up aloft it was easy for her to find the area of parkland behind its perimeter fence. She flew closer. The park was made up of rolling grass country and patches of woodland. There was a large pond at one end. She saw the white deer that gave the Nature Reserve its name. A particularly fine-looking stag seemed to be the most important animal. Kestrel flew over the fence and into the Reserve. She wanted to talk to the stag. An idea had formed in her mind.

Later in the day the animals awoke. They were eager to cover the last bit of ground.

"Come on, Toad," Fox said. "Lead us in."

Toad brought the party to the gap in the fence he remembered so well. The friends were amazed to see a huge collection of animals and birds awaiting their arrival. Kestrel knew all about it, of course, for she had arranged it.

The Great Stag stepped forward. "Welcome to White Deer Park," he said in a deep voice. "The whole countryside around has heard of your exploits. You're all celebrities, you see, and deservedly so. We want to hear all about your adventures when you've time to tell us. But first, come with me, Fox, and bring your friends.

We've prepared a spot for you which can be your quarters until you've made your new homes."

"This is most kind," said Fox, "and we're very grateful."

The animals followed the stag to a sort of hollow where dry grass and bracken had been strewn for their comfort.

"From now on," said Fox, "this will be our meeting-place. It will be just as if we brought with us our own little piece of Farthing Wood."

The animals congratulated each other joyfully. Their great adventure was over.